MW01046398

HEN
HEARS
GOSSIP

By Megan McDonald

Pictures by Joung Un Kim

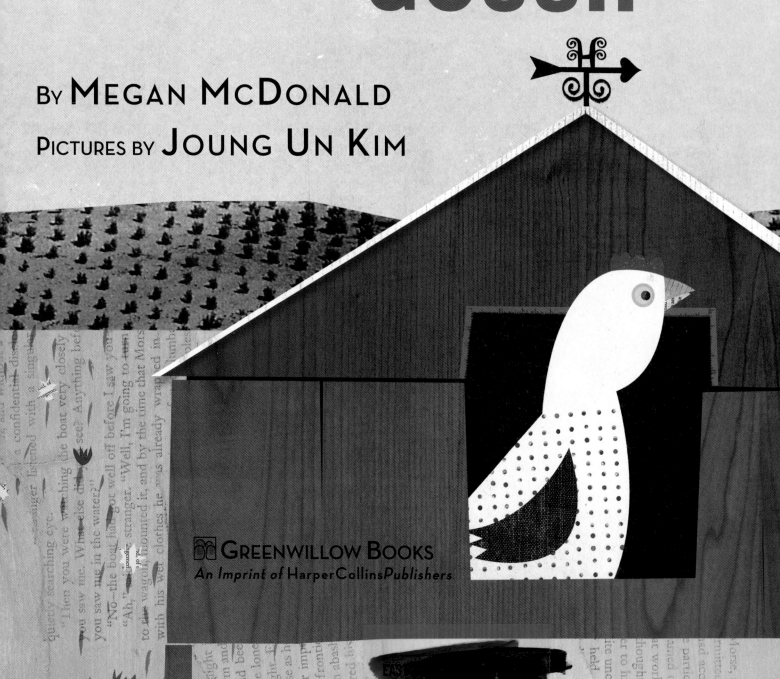

Greenwillow Books
An Imprint of HarperCollinsPublishers

Hen Hears Gossip
Text copyright © 2008 by Megan McDonald
Illustrations copyright © 2008 by Joung Un Kim
All rights reserved. Manufactured in China.
www.harpercollinschildrens.com

Collage and mixed media were used to prepare the full-color art.
The text type is Neutra Text Demi.

Library of Congress Cataloging-in-Publication Data
McDonald, Megan.
Hen hears gossip / by Megan McDonald ;
pictures by Joung Un Kim. — 1st ed.
      p.   cm.

Summary: When Hen overhears some news on the farm,
she runs to tell Duck, who tells another animal, and as
the gossip is repeated from one animal to the next,
it becomes unrecognizable.

ISBN 978-0-06-113876-8 (trade bdg.)
ISBN 978-0-06-113877-5 (lib. bdg.)
[1. Chickens—Fiction. 2. Domestic animals—Fiction.
3. Gossip—Fiction. 4. Communication—Fiction.]
I. Kim, Joung Un, ill. II. Title.
PZ7.M478419He 2008
[E]—dc22 2007027137

First Edition 10 9 8 7 6 5 4 3 2 1

 Greenwillow Books

For my sisters
—M. M.

To Jane Feder
—J. K.

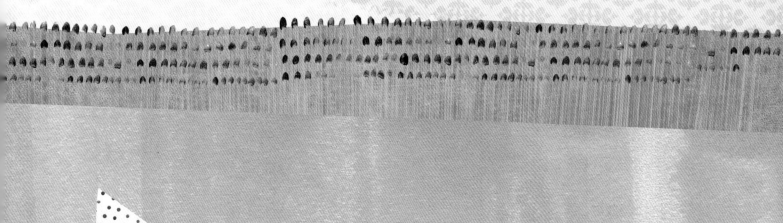
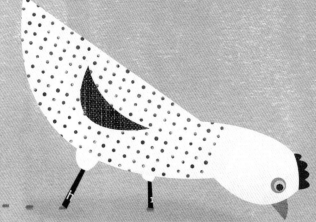

Hen was scratching for bugs
in the barnyard,
by the fence.
"Psst. Psst. Psst."
Pig whispered
something to Cow.
Gossip!
Hen loved gossip!

easy
who

n do much
sizes and, of course
our arrangements. A
der tuberous r

Hen put her ear
up to the fence.
"*Psst. Psst. Psst.*"
Cow whispered something to Pig.
Hen could not wait to tell her friends!

Hen ran to tell Duck.

"Duck! Duck! Sadie the dog has a thorn!"

"WHAT?" said Duck.

Duck ran
to tell Goose.

"Goose! Goose! Daisy the cat grew a horn!"

"WHAT?" said Goose.

Goose ran to tell Turkey.

"Turkey! Turkey! The crazy bat raced a storm!"

"WHAT?" said Turkey.

Turkey ran to tell Hen.

"Hen! Hen! You're lazy, fat, and ate all the corn!"

"WHHAAT?" cried Hen. "I did *NOT* eat all the corn!"

So Hen and Turkey went to look in the barn.
The corn was not eaten.
The corn was in the crib!
"Goose! Goose!" said Turkey. "Why did you say
Hen was lazy, fat, and ate all the corn?"
"I didn't say THAT!
I said, 'The crazy bat raced a storm!'"

Hen and Turkey and Goose looked up at the sky.
The sun was shining.
Not a cloud in sight. *Or* a bat.
"Duck! Duck!" said Goose. "Why did you say
the crazy bat raced a storm?"
"I didn't say THAT!
I said, 'Daisy the cat
grew a horn!'"

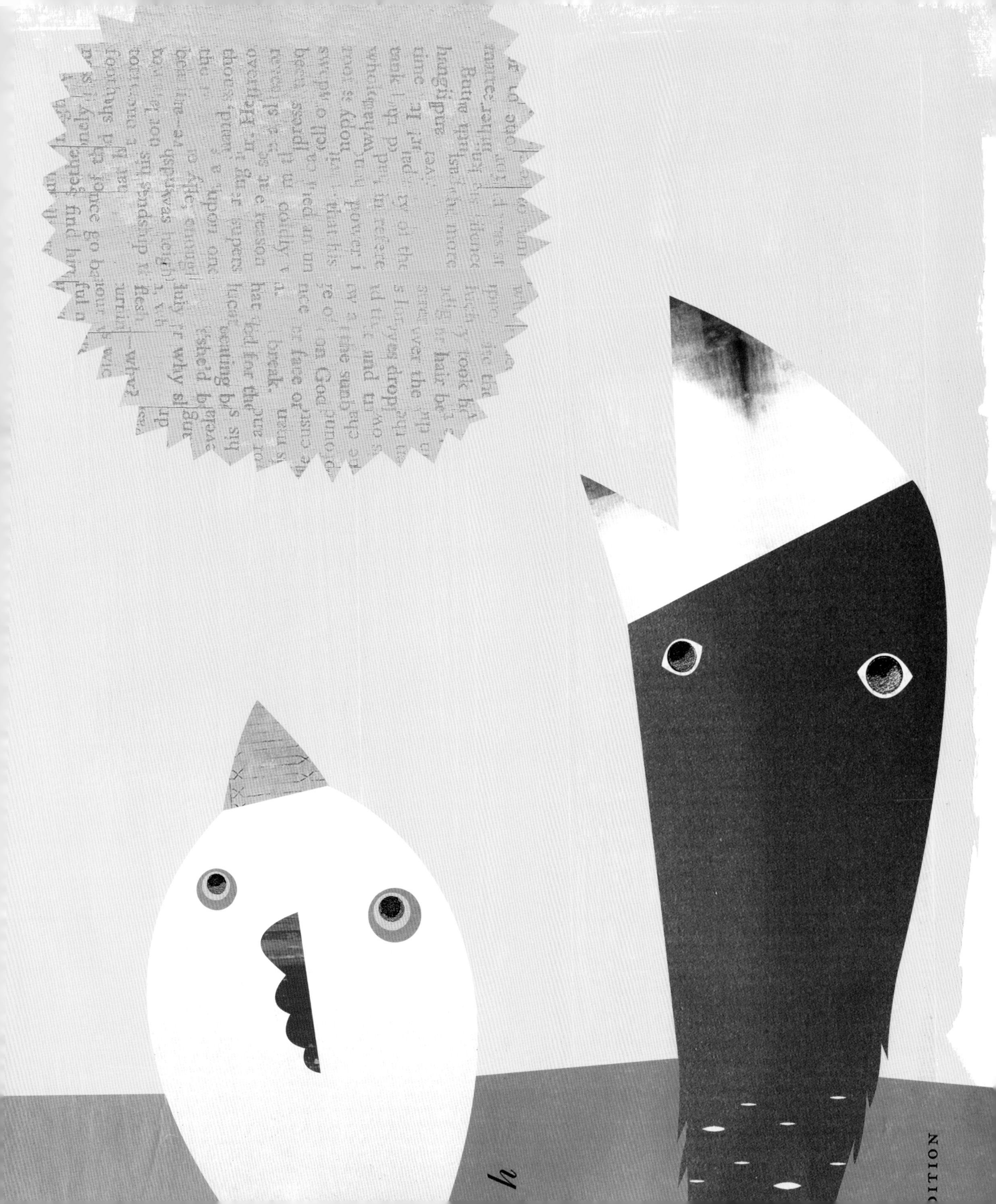

Hen and Turkey, Goose and Duck went
to look for the cat.
Daisy had two pointy ears and two green eyes,
but no horn.
"Hen! Hen!" said Duck. "Why did you say
Daisy the cat grew a horn?"
"I didn't say THAT!
I said, 'Sadie the dog had a thorn!'"

Hen and Turkey, Goose and Duck
went to look for Sadie.
Sadie did not have an itch or a scratch.
Sadie was not in the blackberry patch.
Sadie was on the porch, snoring.
Hen ran to find Cow.

toilet paper, and
environment. It's easy—
5. Recycle everything

"Cow! Cow!" said Hen.
"Why did you tell Pig that Sadie
   the dog had a thorn?"
"I didn't say THAT!
   I said, 'My baby calf was born!'"

A new baby cow! WOW!

Hen called to the others.

"A baby calf was born!"

"A fraidy cat was born?" asked Duck.

"A lazy rat was born?" asked Goose.

"A lady yak was born?" asked Turkey.

"NO! NO! NO!" said Hen.
"NOT a lady yak.
NOT a lazy rat.
NOT a fraidy cat.
A baby CALF was BORN!"
"A baby calf!" said the three.
"Yippee! Let's go see."

Hen and Turkey and Goose and Duck
went to see the new baby.
"Ah," said Goose.
"Oh," said Turkey.
"Kitchee-kitchee koo,"
said Duck.

"Moo," said Hen.